THE POSSESSION
OF NATALIE GLASGOW

HAILEY PIPER

THE POSSESSION OF NATALIE GLASGOW

ISBN: 978-1-0825491-2-0

Cover art copyright © 2019 by Eddie Generous.

THE
POSSESSION
OF
NATALIE
GLASGOW

To J,

Wife, witch, and wonder.

Connecticut, 1976

ೞ

1: The Eyes

A match flared across a white matchbook and lit the end of Heather Glasgow's cigarette. She had managed to quit before Natalie was conceived. Nathaniel drew a line in the sand on that, said he wouldn't put a child in her until "you quit treating your mouth like a goddamn ashtray." Never mind that he smoked his pipe abroad with his friends.

Never mind, because he'd been dead ten months now, because over a decade was a long time between cigarettes, and because after these past two weeks, Heather was entitled to a smoke. She cracked the window of her second floor bedroom and let the cigarette's smoldering end stare into the dusky evening.

"It should be happening by now, shouldn't it?" Margaret Willow asked.

She sat on the end of Heather's king size bed and faced the door, her hands clasped around some gizmo with a microphone taped to the end. She was a stocky woman in her mid-forties, dressed in a black blazer, button-up shirt, and slacks. When she turned to look at Heather, the orange glow of dusk reflected in her slim spectacles.

Supposedly she was a midwife. Heather's sister said she was a witch.

"It's around now," Heather said. She sounded calmer than usual. Witch or midwife, Margaret's presence was reassuring. No one else had stayed in the house overnight these past two weeks. Besides Natalie, of course. Heather didn't think that counted anymore.

Margaret peered close to her gizmo. "I'm not picking up any sound."

"You can't set your watch to her, Ms. Willow, but it'll happen."

"Do you believe there's anything I can do?"

Heather blew smoke through the open

10

window. "I don't, really."

"Do you believe there's anything the doctors can do?"

"She has another test tomorrow. Deep down, I think I've exhausted their capabilities." There was no other reason for Heather to call a woman like Margaret. She glanced down the length of the cigarette. "Will this upset your machines?"

"No, ma'am."

"Then do you want one?"

"It's not my poison of choice, but thank you." Margaret lifted her device and stretched it toward the door.

Heather wondered if she'd feel so relaxed when it actually started. Probably not. Best to take one more drag before she lost her nerve and the cigarette fell out of her trembling hands.

"It feels like when Nate would come home after a week or so away. Some of the time, I mean. Sometimes he'd come home and we'd be over the moon to see him. But some nights, he'd come home from his trips drunk. Went a few rounds with some of his friends on the way home, or with absolute strangers at the airport. I'd wake up hearing him stomp around out there, wait for him to come in and find out if he was angry with me."

Elsewhere in the house, another bed's springs groaned.

Margaret perked up.

Heather dropped her cigarette, as predicted. She picked it up again and snuffed it out in the ashtray. Her hands could scarcely hold onto it even then. Tonight, like every night since the first night, she was sure she would have to wriggle out this window and bust her leg in a jump to the first floor.

At least tonight she wasn't alone. At the very least if Margaret was a weirdo, she was more likely to believe that one of Natalie's nocturnal episodes was a terrifying ordeal.

Natalie's bedroom door creaked open.

"Here's our star." Margaret tilted the device in her hands. "Strong signal."

Heather licked her lips. She could still taste the fallen cigarette. "Could you please not speak?" she asked.

Margaret didn't acknowledge her, just kept her eyes on her device. A black cord ran from the microphone's box to a set of machines where black tape spooled between wheels. Watching Margaret's nervous hands fumble with her machine almost made Heather feel brave.

Natalie's door finished its awful opening cry, and then for the next minute or so there was nothing.

Heather knew the next part was coming. It was the same every night, but she dreaded it all the same.

The hallway floor groaned underfoot. Then again, as Natalie took another step.

Margaret sat up even straighter. Her right eye twitched at every creak in the floor outside, every note that said the wooden boards were sagging under a pensive force. "How much—" She swallowed and forced herself to turn back over her shoulder. "How much does she weigh?"

"She's eleven years old," Heather said. She didn't need to give a specific weight. Whatever set foot out there and made those heavy steps had to be far stronger and heavier than any eleven-year-old girl in the world.

And each step brought it closer. It was the

patient pace of a predator, every movement calculated.

The next footfall landed in front of Heather's bedroom door. The floorboards bent enough that the gap between floor and door widened. Whatever prowled outside pressed itself against the door and set the wood leaning tight against its steel hinges.

Margaret inched backward, deeper into the bed.

"Don't move," Heather whispered. "Don't make a sound."

Margaret clenched her teeth and then pursed her lips. Her hands had gone white, latched around that device. Surely the microphone had captured every groan Natalie pressed into the wood. If it was even Natalie.

The presence held against the door. Then it took another step and the door relaxed, as if it had tensed up in apprehension the same as Margaret and Heather. The creak in the floorboards made a stiff line down the hall.

Heather's heart found its proper rhythm when she heard the first stairway step groan. Natalie was headed downstairs.

Margaret scooted to the edge of the bed. She pulled a handkerchief from the pocket of her blazer and dabbed at her forehead. "I wish I didn't sweat so damn much."

Heather reached for another cigarette. "Was it everything you'd hoped for?"

"I don't hope for this." Margaret shoved her handkerchief back inside her pocket. She was still sweating. "Always, it's better if I'm not needed."

"And are you needed?"

Margaret looked into Heather's eyes. There was no reflection of sunset in those spectacles now, only the clear glass that separated Heather from Margaret's stare. "I think so."

"You're awfully perturbed. I thought it would only be me."

"I'm an expert on this kind of thing, Mrs. Glasgow. I'll tell you something no other expert would. You're never desensitized to the strange. It's always fresh. And when it's scary once, it'll be scary again." Margaret turned to the door. "Have you ever gone out there?"

Heather thought for a moment. "The first

night it happened, I didn't realize it was her. I went out while she was downstairs, thinking it was someone in the house, and went to her room. It was empty, of course. Hurried myself to the stairs, but that's when I saw her. She didn't notice me, but I saw the eyes." She realized she hadn't lit her new cigarette yet. "Imagine that. A mother running from her little girl."

"You did the smart thing. I wish I could do the same." Margaret approached the door and yanked it open.

Heather started up. "You can't!"

"I have to confirm what we're dealing with. Not because I want to. You have to understand that." Margaret's hands wouldn't stop shaking. "It's absolutely not because I want to." And then she left the room, into the hall.

Heather didn't follow. She couldn't even manage to get out of her chair to shut the door.

Margaret would've liked nothing more than to retreat from the hall and lock the bedroom door until morning when, according to Heather, this episode would end.

But how would that help Natalie?

The floor looked worn, but Natalie's path hadn't caused any permanent damage. The stairway to the first floor appeared likewise unharmed. Down below, there came a familiar, sticky click, the opening of a refrigerator door.

Margaret took to the stairs one soft step at a time. Natalie would be distracted by her strange nocturnal diet. Margaret wouldn't get a better chance to perform the church's tests. The Catholic Church was a tedious and overly bureaucratic organization when it came to this kind of problem, but in many regards they were right to be. You couldn't assume what was wrong. There had to be evidence.

The heat hit Margaret as she reached the last couple of steps. There was a dry atmosphere on the first floor of the Glasgow house that hadn't been there when she arrived in the late afternoon to meet Heather in the safety of autumn daylight. This was a blazing summer afternoon. If she spotted steam rise out of Natalie's mouth and nose, she supposed that would be a sign.

Only the ceiling lamp from the upstairs hallway cast any light through the first floor across the living room carpet into the tiled kitchen, but what little Margaret saw made her sweat even worse.

Natalie stood in the kitchen's gloom. She wore a white nightgown. Her hair frizzed at the ends, each strand suffering in the heat. Her skin was flushed and a damp sheen coated her face.

She was rummaging in the fridge, attracted to the bait her mother left for her. Heather said the episodes could go on for five or six hours, but leaving food out seemed to cut the time in half.

Not just any food. Meat, the rarer the better. Heather said it was how her husband used to eat and Natalie had picked up the habit. Only now it was worse, because a few degrees beyond raw seemed too much for her. One morning, Heather found a frozen roast on the floor, still a block of meat-flavored ice, but Natalie had gnawed on its edges anyway.

Margaret could stomach all of that, even the unpleasant sight of Natalie's mouth chewing at shredded red hamburger meat, its gristle painted across her cheeks and chin.

It was the eyes. When Natalie faced the glow

of the fridge they looked normal enough, but if she turned her head even slightly, they were eyes in the dark. Eyes in the dark that reflected the light of the upstairs. Margaret was no biologist, but she knew human eyes didn't do that.

According to the Catholic Church, the skin of one possessed by a demon would burn at the touch of water blessed by an ordained priest. Margaret drew a small, clear vial from her shirt pocket and unscrewed the cap. It would only be a few drops, hardly enough for Natalie to notice she'd been touched.

Unless it burned her, of course. She would notice then. How strong did she have to be to press the floor like that?

Margaret didn't let herself think about it. She swung the vial and droplets sailed toward the kitchen. She tensed her legs to retreat.

Nothing. Natalie grasped another fistful of raw meat and shoved it between her teeth. No burning, but no anger.

Margaret lifted a golden crucifix. All the tests had to be performed, no matter how silly. Or scary. If there was a demon inside Natalie, perhaps it wouldn't care for this symbol. Margaret didn't care for the test, either. She couldn't chuck the crucifix. She had to step into the kitchen and press it to Natalie's skin.

The heat grew worse the closer Margaret came to the fridge. If only that hellish dryness in the air was enough proof, but it wasn't. She readied to bolt. A moment's touch would tell her everything. Just had to be sure she didn't drop the damn thing.

She paused a foot away from Natalie. Drops of sweat raced along her face, around her cheeks, and down her neck. Her fingers were slick, but she kept a stern grip. Now was the time. She pressed the crucifix against Natalie's arm.

Natalie's head turned. Glowing eyes stared up at Margaret's face and a mouthful of meat glistened in the yellow fridge light.

The crucifix didn't affect Natalie, but Margaret didn't notice at first because of the sound. It was almost worse than the creaking, too-heavy footsteps upstairs. No, it was worse, she decided. Much worse.

A clicking, guttural groan slid through

Natalie's throat and chest. It made her whole body tense and quake, like a muscle flexing itself into overexertion. The tremor spread through the kitchen and shook the food inside the fridge, the glasses in the cupboards, the pots and pans, the windows. It shook the crucifix out of Margaret's hands and the bones up her arm, through the rest of her body. She understood the sound and backed away from the little girl.

Natalie growled and the kitchen growled with her.

Margaret almost cried out when something touched her from behind. Just the stairway's banister. She grasped it tight. She hadn't even noticed her retreat from the kitchen.

Natalie glanced at the crucifix on the floor tile, and then returned her attention to the hamburger meat.

Church doctrine expected that the demonically possessed might speak in foreign tongues such as Aramaic or older. Margaret couldn't call that growl a proper language, but she felt if a priest was here with her, he would've counted it as a bad sign.

But the holy water and the crucifix had failed. There would be no help from the church.

Margaret turned to the stairs and started a slow climb. She supposed there was good and bad news so far in this case. Demonic possession could be ruled out. Now that only left every other possibility.

The first step creaked beneath her.

Margaret didn't turn her head. If she turned her head, she would've seen too clearly, and then she would've run, and then—she didn't want to know what would've happened then. Instead, she glanced out the corner of her eye toward the kitchen, her face unmoved from its attention on the stairway.

Natalie had left the fridge. The door hung ajar, its light showing only the abandoned plastic package and the hamburger meat that now leaked red fluid across the kitchen tiles. She had crossed the space between the kitchen, across the carpet and stone floor underneath, up to the bottom of the stairs without a sound, and only her first footfall on that creaky bottom step had given her away.

She was two steps behind Margaret.

A stillness took over. Margaret thought of a deer in headlights, but that analogy felt off. She was a deer in the woods, separated from her herd, while a creature fierce and terrible loomed over her.

Natalie was just a child. Eleven years old. Margaret guessed she outweighed her four times.

But there was something in her that growled at such a pitch that it made the kitchen tremble, that stepped so hard it made the house cry for mercy. Margaret knew there was only a small, rail-thin child behind her, but she likewise knew she wasn't as strong as a house. What lived inside Natalie could buckle her. It could break her.

Her eye fixed on that refrigerator, on the raw hamburger it illuminated.

Her hand slid up the banister, grasped firm, and she ascended two steps at once this time. Her leg carried her up. She reached for the step after the next. A little farther along the banister. It took every ounce of self-control not to charge up those steps as fast as she could, as if some primal animal fear lived inside her, perhaps all humans, a scrap of prey's panic from days long past.

The steps below creaked again. Natalie was patient. What was inside her, it knew it had given itself away with that first step. It had ears, after all. Natalie's ears.

The top of the steps wasn't too far away. Running on the stairs was death. Margaret just had to keep that in mind. If she ran, Natalie wouldn't follow with cautious, predatory steps. She would chase.

Margaret's foot hit the top of the steps. Her hand left the banister in one slippery motion and reached for the corner wall. She felt the stillness coming again, an uncertainty of what to do now that she was past the steps, and a certainty that to freeze here would be a mistake. She dragged her back foot off the previous step, toward the top. Natalie was four steps below. She would have to ascend. Margaret had a straight shot to Heather's bedroom, where the door still hung wide open.

She heard another creak. Natalie wasn't going to wait for a decision.

Margaret took another step, and as she did, slipped her arms out of her blazer. Another step and she thrust it behind her without looking. Then she ran. She had to hope the flying blazer would distract Natalie, or that whatever hid inside Natalie's skin hadn't expected Margaret to run.

She didn't hear anything at first. Then the steps creaked, a low rumble filled the space between the floors of the Glasgow house, and the steps groaned, the floorboards groaned, Natalie was on the second floor, chasing. Right behind her. About to grab her. Faster.

Heather's hand stuck out from her doorway and yanked Margaret inside. The door slammed shut. Heather and Margaret shoved against it, and it swelled against them. The presence outside insisted they let it in. Its growl rattled the doorknob, the hallway air. It didn't try to break the door down. Maybe it only understood Natalie's bedroom doorknob, not others. Maybe that was how Heather had kept it inside the house these past many nights.

The swelling eased a little, and then all the way. Heavy footfalls crossed the hall at the same deliberate pace as when Natalie first opened her bedroom door tonight. They stalked up the hallway, past Natalie's bedroom, toward the upstairs bathroom.

Heather and Margaret didn't move from the door in case their steps might give them away. Margaret could hardly see the door itself. Her spectacles had fogged a little near Natalie and been tussled when running. They needed cleaning. Margaret wished she could clean away the vision of Natalie's reflective eyes and the abandoned hamburger meat. How close she had been to those things.

Natalie neared the door again. The floor cried, but she let the door be this time. She passed them, down the hall, back down the stairs again. Soon she would be on the floor, her hands quick to stuff raw meat in her mouth.

Heather eased away from the door, back to her chair by the window. An unlit cigarette awaited her in the crook of the ashtray.

Margaret knelt beside the bed and laid her head against the comforter. Her breathing rocked her chest up and down. "I have news, at least."

"Good news?" Heather asked, hand on her heart. "Or just news?"

"Your daughter isn't possessed by a demon."

Heather paused. "Then she's crazy?"

"No, ma'am."

"Well, does she have a brain lesion? A disease? What is it? What's wrong with her?"

"Please keep your voice down," Margaret said. She could see relief in Heather's face, not because of any diagnosis. It had to be comforting to know someone else was just as afraid as she'd been these last couple weeks. "The Catholic Church's tests ruled out a demon. There's still something inside her."

"But you don't know what?"

"I may need to run different tests." Margaret's hands trembled. Even the idea of getting near Natalie again in this state sounded insane.

Heather at last lit her cigarette. "Now you sound like a doctor."

"Let me have a chance to think, Mrs. Glasgow. This isn't the medical field. They wouldn't have been able to help her."

"Why not? Because you can? You say something's inside her, but you don't know what it is. It could be a growth they couldn't detect before or a sickness—" Heather stuck the cigarette between her lips and inhaled deep. There was something she wanted to say, a crazy idea of her own, that she was too ashamed to utter aloud. Or too afraid.

Sometime past midnight, Natalie shambled back to her room. She didn't shut the door, but Margaret heard the bedsprings. She opened Heather's door only briefly to see if the coast was clear. Unrelenting heat breathed from Natalie's bedroom and filled the hall with that oppressive summer day air. Margaret crept through to close Natalie's door. Even the doorknob was warm.

"I'll be back tomorrow afternoon, after your bring Natalie home from her doctor," Margaret said. "We'll go over the recordings once I've had some sleep."

"You're going to drive this late?" Heather asked. "After what you've been through?"

"I'll sleep better not being in this house." Margaret adjusted her spectacles. "I didn't mean that to sound rude. I never do. Just, keep your door locked in case she gets up again. I'll try to learn what I can. You do the same, in your own way."

"In my own way," Heather echoed. Margaret

had a funny way of saying she disagreed.

ஐ

2: Doctors

It took Heather over half a dozen handshakes before Dr. Liam Horne had introduced to her every brilliant man he'd gathered to himself today in his research facility at the Stamford campus. Heather couldn't remember any of their names.

Liam then addressed the room. "If everyone would approach the glass, we're about to begin."

The brilliant men approached the glass, some dressed in black or gray suits, some dressed in white lab coats, most of them in spectacles that made Heather think of Margaret. She had looked to have a keener eye than anyone present, but looks could be deceiving. These men were renowned in their fields, and Margaret? What exactly was Margaret's field of expertise?

"I appreciate your patience, Mrs. Glasgow," Liam said. "By now, I think a woman of less fortitude, without her husband at her side, might've done something drastic."

"Drastic?" Heather asked, as if to say, *Little old me? Drastic? Never!*

"You know, consulted a fortune teller, maybe the church, or worse, one of those smoke and juju healers. Forget I said anything. Not the kind of idea I'd expect would cross a sophisticated mind like yours, what with your husband being who he was. Damn, I miss that man."

Heather should've said something encouraging, that Nathaniel spoke fondly of Liam Horne, that he always meant to invite him on another hunting trip. Those would've been nice things to say. They weren't true. Nathaniel hardly gave Liam a second thought beyond that he was the family physician, but they were nice things. Heather didn't have space in her mind for nice things. She only had space for Natalie.

So Heather said nothing and watched her daughter through the glass.

32

Natalie lay strapped to a white table, her head stuck in a white cylinder. Supposedly the room was too radioactive to step inside, yet not so radioactive that she was in any danger. Heather didn't understand that, but she wasn't about to ask.

"It's mapping," Liam said. An eerie glow crossed the room beyond the glass.

"How much did you sedate her?" one of the doctors asked.

"We didn't. Part of her condition is sleep to a near-sedated extent."

"And there's nothing physically wrong?"

"We'll learn soon enough."

Heather found herself wringing her hands and lowered them to her sides, where they began to wring her dress. She had never hoped for a machine to find something wrong with her little girl before today. But today came after two hellish weeks of useless Dr. Horne, of befuddled specialists, of tests that all came back saying Natalie was perfectly fine. A basic mercury thermometer couldn't even tell Natalie's temperature was up. It was enough to make Heather scream bloody murder each time she returned to her car, while Natalie dozed away in the passenger seat.

Only Margaret seemed to understand.

It took an hour to have the results of the scan, a layout of Natalie's brain. Who she was and what she thought, every piece of her mapped out on those scans. Liam and his brilliant men groomed the results with their eyes, their spectacles, and their magnifying glasses, the little ones that too many doctors seemed to carry in their pockets where men used to keep their pocket watches. They muttered to each other, a dull rumble of speculation.

"Well?" Heather asked. "What's wrong with her?"

The murmur quieted in an instant. The men glanced at each other, glanced at Liam, as if to ask why he'd brought them here when he already had all the answers.

"Please understand, Mrs. Glasgow." Liam held up his hands in a placating gesture. "These scans—the brain is the most complex organ in the human body, perhaps the most complex organ in all biology. It can take time to go over in detail and find exactly what's causing the problem."

"But you must have a hint." The back of Heather's neck burned. She wondered if a thermometer could detect *that*. "There must be something that doesn't look right. Right? I could understand if it was just one little thing wrong with her, or even one big thing, but all these problems, all of it together, her brain should be the Rockefeller Center Christmas Tree of problems, and you can't find even one—"

Heather stopped all at once. She stared at a room of ghastly faces, growing older and more obsolete by the moment. These were brilliant men? These men thought they could help her daughter? She couldn't see it. All she saw was a look of shamed confusion that scurried in their eyes, every one of them. They were pitiable, almost children. Yes, that's it. School children who didn't know the teacher's answer, each of them taking center stage in class only to be ridiculed, and then cry for their mothers.

She looked on them with motherly eyes and spoke in a motherly, doting tone. "You don't know anything, do you? None of you do. None of you know anything at all."

3: The Study

Margaret chuckled to herself. "And the horse he rode in on?" she asked. She had just returned to the Glasgow house and heard an earful.

Heather covered her mouth and coughed out a laugh. "They didn't want to help her. The doctor brought them to show off his unique find." She kept her mouth covered through a yawn. "You'd think I would sleep through the day, being up these nights. I'll get in an hour here or there, but it's, you know." She let her voice trail off.

"But you have nightmares?" Margaret pulled a checkered notebook from her bag and sat in a tall chair, cushioned with red leather. It was Nathaniel's favorite chair, with the tall back to cradle the ghastly height of him. "I had one, too."

Heather seated herself on the sofa across the coffee table. "What was it?"

"I'm not sure." Margaret adjusted her spectacles and crossed her legs. She came off as much more confident in the daylight, without having to toy with her machine or escape an eleven-year-old. "Usually my dreams are visual. I'll remember images of them, like my brain takes a vacation through them and keeps a photo album. This was different. It was all feelings. I remember it was hot and I was afraid." Her eyes were wet behind her spectacles. "And angry. The kind of angry that makes you upset, like you'd never wish to have something worth being so angry about."

Heather couldn't have put her nightmares into those words, but Margaret described them almost exactly. "I have seen things, at least the past three nights. I can't tell what. There's a tree, but not like the pines we have outside. It's a strange tree. And there's meat on the ground. A shadow."

"You've been exposed longer." Margaret's pen danced along her notebook. "If we wait even a few more days, we might get a clearer picture."

"We can't wait." Heather's nails scraped at the sofa. She wished she could smoke down here. Part of her almost had yesterday. Nathaniel was gone, and so was Natalie, it seemed. No, she had to hope Natalie was coming back. "She needs to get better."

"For that to happen, I have to know what happened to her. What was the start of this? Before the first night, I mean."

"Oh, there was a morning she was at the fridge, asking for meat. I told her I'd make her breakfast and she only ate her sausage. I thought she was being picky."

Margaret tapped her pen against her notebook. Asking a client what happened was much like a doctor dealing with a patient. A patient could already know what they're doing wrong and just needed the right questions to pry it out.

"I'm having a rough time breathing, doc."

"Well, are you still smoking?"

"Yup, two packs a day. Why do you ask?"

Heather was a proud client. Margaret expected she and her husband were similar in that sense, but her husband died long before Natalie's condition set in, and so never had to experience his resolve being whittled away night after night. Experiences like these could break anyone eventually. Sooner if it was your own child. Right now, Natalie slept upstairs, where she couldn't hurt anyone. That would change by nightfall.

"Heather, I want you to really think hard, back to before it got bad. Did anything strange happen earlier that day? That week? Something out of the ordinary. A place Natalie wouldn't normally go, a person she might've spoken with? Something new or different. It would've given you pause."

Heather sat quiet for a moment. Then her eyes lit up and her mouth twitched. There was an unpleasant thought inside her that demanded it be unleashed, it was plain to see on her face. She worked her lips past it. "The study." She left the sofa.

Margaret hurried to catch up with her at the end of the first floor hall.

"I only open it up when I'm cleaning." Heather reached a set of double doors, so thin you could punch through them. "I keep it the way he left it. It didn't seem right to move anything."

"Of course."

She reached over the doors and retrieved a small iron key. "We only took a couple things from inside to bury him with, like his favorite hat, a photo of us, you know. Other than that, his study stays locked. Sometimes I dust and vacuum. No one else sets foot inside."

Margaret stepped closer. "Except?"

"I must've forgotten to lock it after I vacuumed last month. I don't know. It's been a rough time. I don't even remember if I closed the doors." Heather slid the key into the lock. "When I passed through the hall again, Natalie was in there." The flimsy doors swung open without a touch.

The air hit Margaret before the sight of Nathaniel's study. It carried a man's stink, even after all these months. It also carried scents of dirt and must and preserving chemicals, of animal hair and wood finish.

And there was a weight in the air. Margaret didn't consider herself any kind of medium, but she expected that after last night's encounter, her body would at least recognize a similar sensation. There was foreboding here, a presence that lived in the space of a dead man, so obvious and disquieting that even a layman like Heather could feel it. It was obvious in the way she shuddered when the doors finished opening. She led the way inside.

Margaret closed the doors of the study behind them. There was a risk that they might lock on their own, perhaps if the Glasgow house was haunted, but she thought not. Only one person here was haunted. Besides, they really were flimsy doors. She didn't want the atmosphere here to go floating around the halls and up the stairs. Better to be mired in it. Let it get to know her.

To the left of the door, she found Nathaniel's desk, where he displayed a fisher that had been handled by a taxidermist. He had also displayed a photo of a hunt. Margaret leaned in for a closer look.

It was a photo of Nathaniel himself, and he looked exactly as his study suggested him to Margaret, the spitting image of an archaic great white hunter, some relic of an imperial century past. He was a stiff-necked, bald-headed man with a sharp, hawkish nose. Margaret half-expected to see a generic safari hat in one hand, but instead he held a hat sewn of golden fur. He wore a white shirt with rolled-up sleeves, brown khakis, and leather boots surely made from some creature he'd killed. Margaret didn't know anything about guns, but Nathaniel's looked big enough to bring down a rhino. Under his boot lay a dead wildebeest.

The man enjoyed his hunting.

The animals of the study told their own bloody story. They were impossible to ignore, with their glass orbs staring from where eyes once stared. There were typical remains that Margaret expected to see in the trophy room of a hunter, like the mounted head of a North American deer, a red fox, a stuffed mallard with its green head and white collar. Then there were more unusual trophies, such as the head of a black bear, the standing fisher on the desk, a wolverine.

And there were exotics, like elephant tusks, a rhino's horn, and the heads of a giraffe, a dingo, and others. Margaret wasn't sure all of these were legal, but the hunter was beyond the law now. Nathaniel Glasgow's pride gazed glassily from the center of the wall that faced opposite the door, where he mounted the heads of a timber wolf, a lioness, a boar far larger than Margaret had ever seen, and a crocodile skin that stretched from wall to wall just beneath the ceiling.

"I know what it looks like," Heather said. "A man this violent out in the world, he must've been violent at home. I shouldn't have told you about his coming home drunk. It paints an unfair picture. He never hurt us. Nate was a hard man, but not a cruel man."

Margaret didn't know enough about him to say she was wrong, but cruel or not, he was merciless. "Where was Natalie?"

Heather pointed to the center of the room. "Right there, on the floor. She was sitting and staring. I didn't pay attention. I just stormed in, grabbed her, and hauled her out." She pressed the heel of her hand against her forehead. "Jesus, I gave her an earful. And for what? She didn't deserve it, just for that. She misses her father. Christ, what's wrong with me?"

"Mrs. Glasgow." Margaret pulled Heather's arms to her sides and looked over her spectacles into Heather's eyes. "It's not worth beating yourself up over. We can't change the past. Believe me, there are plenty of little things I let eat at me at night, but when it comes to helping someone, we have to put all that shit away, pardon my English. Let's help Natalie now, yes?"

Heather nodded. That other thing that was bothering her hounded her eyes and carved her skin into a wrinkled map of countries and states and counties. She lowered her face into Margaret's shoulder and loud sobs quaked through her body.

Margaret held her. "Mrs. Glasgow, did you ever go with your husband on these trips?"

Heather shook her head.

"Besides the animals, did he ever bring anything else back with him? Coins, dolls, masks, the kinds of things—" Margaret cut herself off before she could say, anything that a spirit might attach itself to, as if Heather would know. As if Heather was in the right place of mind to hear such a thing.

"In the desk," Heather managed through a

45

sob. She pulled herself away from Margaret and covered her face. "I'm sorry."

"Please don't be." Many people looked to Margaret for comfort, often after delivery and especially when things went wrong. She never seemed to get any better at it, but she supposed if they kept looking then she couldn't be doing too badly either.

She opened the top drawer of Nathaniel's desk. Stone arrowheads pointed accusingly at her. Ancient coins stared from glass cases. The next drawer held a small mask made of clay, its expression frozen in laughter. The idea that artifacts of another culture carried an inherently demonic presence was ethnocentrism at work, Margaret knew, but something angry could have hitched a ride with Heather's husband. And then poor Natalie.

Margaret glanced back at his photo on the desk. Greedy, repulsive man. Just what did you bring into your home?

The photo didn't answer.

"You can stop," Heather said. She seemed to have composed herself.

Margaret looked up. "Stop?"

"You can stop looking. I know what it is. I think I knew it last night when we were talking. It didn't occur to me before, maybe because I'd been hoping it was a demon or a lesion. Can you imagine? Wishing that for my own daughter."

"Mrs. Glasgow—"

"It's Nathaniel."

Margaret gently closed the drawer. She had to choose her tone carefully so as not to sound derisive, especially because she didn't mean to be. "You suspect Nathaniel's ghost?"

"It feels like him. He'd always eat his meat as rare as he could. When he was drunk he'd stomp around the halls like she does every night. That heaviness and strength."

"And the anger?"

Heather lowered her head. "I must've done something wrong. With the funeral or, I don't know. Since then."

"Let's not jump to conclusions," Margaret said. She stepped around the desk and opened the study doors. She was ready to be free of this place. "We have tests for that, too. We can find out if it's

Nathaniel through a séance. He's likely to be much less dangerous than a demon."

Heather followed Margaret out of the study. "How long would it take to get one of those ready?"

"A séance? A week, maybe, to bring my contacts together. Maybe by then your dreams will—"

"No." Heather yanked the doors shut and thrust the iron key into the lock. "If you had to get him out of her, how long would it take to be ready? If you knew for certain."

"I could do that myself." Margaret swallowed. "I could do it tonight. But it's a ceremony that draws out whatever's inside her. It'd be dangerous to do that without knowing for certain what it is. We might not be prepared."

"I don't care."

"You can't mean that."

"I don't care about the danger, Ms. Willow, because I care too much about Natalie. We can't keep going like this, waiting and testing." Heather brushed past Margaret, back down the hall, and grasped the stairway banister. "Follow me upstairs. I need to show you something in Natalie's room."

Margaret recoiled as if the sun had set preemptively and Natalie now stalked the halls of the Glasgow house. But the sun hadn't set yet. That would be another couple of hours still. Margaret didn't have an excuse. She followed Heather up the stairs.

Heather wasn't quiet or subtle about opening Natalie's bedroom door. In the day, Natalie was no danger. She was just a young girl in a lot of trouble. The window hung wide open, letting in an autumn breeze, but Heather would have to shut and lock it before nightfall.

Margaret couldn't help but like her room. The walls wore faded magenta paint and parts of them hid behind pencil sketches of different animals. Natalie approached the wilderness with a kinder attitude than her father.

"Come here," Heather said. She stood to one side of the bed.

Natalie lay in a new nightgown. Her skin remained flushed, like last night. A bag of ice lay half-melted beside her head. The air here was cool. It seemed the heat only spread and infected the world after sunset, but Natalie was stuck with it around the clock.

"I get her up to drink every hour or so. She'll use the bathroom." Heather ran her hands through Natalie's damp hair. "Nathaniel inside her is getting stronger, but that's not a physical thing. Natalie, her body, is getting weaker. The force of it, the heat, the … diet. It's wringing her out, running her ragged. She sleeps through the day, but it's the sleep of nightmares. She's not going to make it much longer. And neither will I."

Margaret could see it. Heather's eyes were bloodshot. The lines on her face were bold and deep.

"I can't lose them both," Heather went on. "And especially not because of each other. Please, Ms. Willow. Margaret. I need your help. I'll do anything, but please, it has to be as soon as possible."

Margaret turned her attention from Heather to the bed. Natalie's breathing was shallow, raspy. She might have had the strongest lungs in the world, but the nights were taking their toll. This thing inside her, Nathaniel or otherwise, was going to dry her out and walk the poor girl to her death. She might've had any number of parasites swimming through her digestive system for all the raw meat she'd consumed. Eleven years of life weren't enough to withstand all this.

Between mother and daughter, everything they were going through, and the fragility of their lives together—what else was Margaret supposed to say?

She clasped her hands together. "I'll be here before dark. But you have to do everything exactly as I say, no matter what."

Heather agreed.

CB

4: Belladonna

None of Margaret's colleagues could appear on short notice. She had expected this. Of course, if she could gather more people last minute, she would've opted for the séance instead. Going solo was another reason not to perform the exorcism yet, if you wanted to call it that. Margaret wouldn't. An exorcism was an expulsion. What she planned to do was more about enticing the intruding presence so that it would manifest outside of the host.

That was what made it so dangerous not to know for certain that Nathaniel was in there.

Heather eyed Margaret's leather bag, now swollen with ritual ingredients. "We're not going to hurt her, are we? I don't think I could hurt her."

Margaret considered a lie, that yes, this would hurt her, and they should wait until Nathaniel's presence could be confirmed. The time for that lie would've been this afternoon, before she surrendered to Heather's pleas.

"Don't worry about Natalie. We're only here to help her. You should worry more about you and me. Natalie already has this thing inside her. When we draw it out, we expose ourselves to it."

"It's only Nate."

"I hope you're right. I really do." Margaret crossed the den and led the way to the double doors of Nathaniel's study. "Is she inside? Is she prepared?"

Heather followed close behind. "I did everything you said." She stepped next to Margaret. "Did we have to wait for sunset?"

"It emerges on its own then. I'm hoping if it's already at the surface, it'll be easier to coax forward." Easier on Natalie, at least. Herself and Heather Glasgow? She didn't think anything would lighten their burden tonight. She turned to Heather. "You don't have to be here for this."

"I suppose not. This isn't my world." Heather

pressed open the double doors. "But how could I leave her?"

Natalie lay balled up across the study from the doors, against the wall. Heather had followed Margaret's instructions. She brought Natalie down here, and then laid some of her favorite things around her, some bits of jewelry, a patched-up horsey doll Natalie had probably kept since she was a toddler, and a couple of her most recent drawings. They were to remind her of herself. Hopefully Nathaniel would be more attracted to his own study than his daughter's personal possessions.

Just as important, a glass of salt sat in front of these objects. It was to protect Natalie in case the entity was not her father and might mean to untether itself from her by violence if necessary.

"I only did as instructed," Heather said. "Nothing more. I didn't even restrain her."

"You did perfect." Margaret squeezed Heather's shoulder. "Now let me do my part."

First, there was another dose of salt to add to the room. Margaret closed the double doors, set her bag down, and retrieved a jar filled with white crystals and powder. She shook a line of it along the doorway, and then walked around the center of the study. When she was done, a circle of salt lay between the doors and Natalie.

Heather set her teeth. "Is this witchcraft?"

"These are old practices. Some of them are old as the Roman rites of exorcism. Some, much older." Margaret returned the jar to her bag and drew out five green candles. "You can call them witchcraft if that helps you. A doctor doesn't worry where the methods came from. A doctor wants to heal a patient." She stood the five candles around the circle. "Could I borrow your matchbook, Mrs. Glasgow?"

Heather slipped it from the fold in her dress, where she once also kept cigarettes a lifetime ago, and handed the small white square to Margaret. "Heather. Please."

Margaret lit the five candles. "Thank you, Heather." She returned the matchbook and then returned to her bag. She was nearly done. Next she drew out the largest item, a bundle of cuttings from a spruce tree. "Spruce wood makes smoke. A lot of smoke." She wrestled with her explanation.

Heather seemed a sharp woman, but how could you begin to explain to anyone the impermeability of the world? "We need to create what I'd call a vague space. Smoke obscures the senses. We lay that obfuscation between life and death. In smoke and fog, the spirit can roam."

Heather licked her lips. "I don't suppose I can smoke in here myself?"

"Nathaniel made you quit, didn't he? If we present him something he dislikes, I'm not sure we'll succeed."

"It would sure help my nerves."

Margaret used one of the candles to light the spruce ends. It didn't take much to get them going, but she waved her hand over them and helped the smoke to billow. Soon it wafted across the circle and began to rise.

Last of all, Margaret retrieved a clay saucer from the bag and laid a handful of leafy herbs across the top. Then she laid the saucer in the center of the circle. "Belladonna. Better known as deadly nightshade. This is our key."

"Should I get something of his?"

Margaret looked around. "We're surrounded

by his things. He should be comfortable here." Peaceful and pliable, Margaret hoped.

"But maybe there's something missing."

"Only if we find out there's something of his that he wants, that's holding him to the world of the living. Otherwise, I don't want to confuse him. If we make a mistake, pick the wrong object, it might remind him of his mortality." Margaret coughed. She never got used to the smoke. "It could repel him. Make him angry, frighten him, send him back into Natalie, turn him from us. We want to draw him out and make him agreeable."

"Finish his business and go." Heather glanced around the room. "He died in his sleep. The autopsy said it was heart failure, what you'd call a natural consequence of living the kind of life he did. I don't know what I could've done better."

"You'll get to ask him in a minute. The sun is almost set."

Margaret already felt that tremble in her hands. Last night she could hardly hold her microphone. Now she was supposed to perform a ceremony, a rushed one. Everything had been such a tumult since then that she hadn't had time to listen through her recordings. Tonight could be the same brand of mistake, of Natalie standing behind her on the stairway of the Glasgow house. Natalie, growling, hungry, strong. Here she would wake up and there would be no doors between them.

Natalie stirred. First she uncurled against the wall. Her back curved and her arms stretched in front of her. The yawn was almost a growl itself.

The smoke clouded Margaret's vision and she had to wipe her spectacles. It was getting almost too thick for the spruce bundle to have made on its own. Nathaniel's study lay mired in a gray cloud, broken only by the gentle light of the branches and the circle of candles. The spruce bundle stood on one end and burned from its top. The fire would take some time to reach the carpet. If the drawing of the spirit took that long, Margaret expected she and Heather would already be dead.

Natalie began to rise. Every movement was deliberate, a subtle stretch of the leg, a gentle rolling in the shoulders. She was in no hurry to stand. Her head turned slow from side to side. The smoke had confused whatever dwelled inside her. There was another growl, but softer now, curious.

"Aren't you supposed to say something?" Heather whispered.

Margaret meant to say something, just that in the heat and intensity, she was having a hard time finding her tongue. It was in there, somewhere.

"Spirit," she said, and then choked on her words. It had to be the smoke. And nerves. And fear. "Spirit, enter our sacred space. Let us speak with you and offer comfort."

Natalie's throat rumbled. She began to pace the far wall. The floor creaked beneath each pensive step. She couldn't see Margaret too well, certainly couldn't smell her, but could she tell the direction of Margaret's voice? Margaret wondered if she should pace as well, but her legs threatened to quit on her at any moment. They were as shaky as her hands.

"Spirit, I know you're here with us." Margaret took a step toward Nathaniel's desk. "Come forward in this place of life and death. Here, we are one." She turned to Heather. "If there's something you want to say to him, say it."

Heather wiped at her eyes. "Nate? It's me. It's Heather. Do you recognize my voice?"

Natalie continued to pace. The smoke thickened, made her harder to see. Margaret could only make out the suggestion of an eleven-year-old girl on the other side of Nathaniel's study.

"Nate, I've missed you." Heather took a step deeper into the room, her foot at the edge of the salt circle. "We both have, Natalie and I. God, it's been hard without you. Some mornings I wake up and forget you're dead, like maybe you're off on one of your hunting trips and you'll be home next week. Then I remember and it's like you've died all over again. Stupid, I know. It gets easier—no, not easier. But each time it happens hurts a little less than the last time."

Margaret thought she saw movement beside Natalie, a leg much thicker than hers that kept in stride. When she paced back, nothing. Margaret wiped her spectacles for the twentieth time since morning. At next glance, there was no mistake. Something walked with Natalie in the smoke.

"But then you started this insanity with Natalie. Nate, she doesn't deserve it. It's destroying her life. Whatever I did wrong, don't take it out on her. Please, tell me what to do to make it right."

Natalie didn't seem to notice her mother or the thing that walked with her. It moved as she moved, a puppeteer and its puppet. For these past weeks, it had been a formless spirit that dwelled in Natalie's flesh, but here in the smoke, with the worlds obscured, it was a creature made manifest, not quite dead, not quite alive, not quite physical, not quite immaterial.

And every time Natalie moved one leg, it moved two. Not quite human, then.

"I'll do anything. But let Natalie go. Let's fix this, like we used to do. Happy family, strong family. Right?"

But it wasn't a demon. It couldn't be a demon, not when the holy water and the crucifix did nothing, so that meant it was something else, but it was not Nathaniel. An entirely different thing. Not Nathaniel.

"Heather, stop!" Margaret snapped.

The growl rattled through Natalie's throat, same as it did last night, and coursed through the walls, across Nathaniel's prizes, and within the sleek form that slid through the smoke, across the circle of salt.

Heather's spine stiffened. "Nate?"

Margaret grasped her arm and pulled her close just as the presence lunged. One of the double doors shattered and the spirit in the smoke doubled back toward the salt circle. Margaret pulled Heather alongside Nathaniel's desk. Another rumble ripped through the study.

Not a growl this time, but a roar.

When the form charged again, Margaret wasn't fast enough. It knocked into the desk and Heather at once. She cried out and tumbled toward the wall across from the door. Margaret fell to one side, out of her way, almost into Natalie, who continued her pacing as if none of this was happening. Margaret turned back toward Nathaniel's desk.

Now she saw it clearly, almost there. Almost alive. Dead, spirit, here it didn't matter. In the smoke, all was one. She'd said so herself. Real, present, dangerous.

The shoulders and back stretched so taut that the hair on its back jutted up like spines. Four legs stood atop Nathaniel's desk, their muscles tensed solid as bone. A tail swung behind the hind legs, long and coated in a bush of hair at the tip. Golden cat eyes stared through the fog, as if they could see clear as day, above a mouth cursed into a black frown. That frown parted and the flesh peeled away from curved, sharp teeth.

The lioness's roar sent the study rumbling again, a quake hard enough to knock Nathaniel's trophies off the walls. Margaret's spectacles trembled off her face. In the ever-worsening haze, she only made out the form by the lioness's golden fur. She was much larger than a lioness looked in photographs. The heat was immense, the oppression of a hot day stalking prey in the grasslands. Some prey animal, unsuspecting, hopeless. Trapped in her gaze.

She turned her cat's eyes to Heather, prone on the floor, who didn't make a sound. Then she stepped off the desk, her maw hanging open.

"No!" Margaret couldn't see, could barely catch her breath, but she could still manage a shriek. "Get me! Here! I'm the one who got away!"

The lioness growled yet again. Her next step

passed over Heather's legs.

Margaret almost giggled. Her distraction had worked. And now what? She looked around for one of Nathaniel's hunting rifles, but couldn't see anything and hadn't used one in ten years. And then, would it do any good?

She fumbled behind her for something, anything, an object to thrust at the lioness, and never took her eyes off that golden stare. The fiery spruce might have worked if she could find it. The shattered study door would help clear the smoke, but not fast enough. Her hand found a solid chunk of wood, heavy enough that she could fool herself into believing she might fight off four hundred pounds of muscled predator.

She swiped in front of her. "Spirit, you're not welcome here!"

The lioness's throat quaked. She stepped to one side, into the salt circle. Her back arched, the forelegs outstretched. She was about to pounce.

Margaret shoved her weapon in front of her, now a shield.

The lioness hissed. Margaret hadn't ever heard a sound like that from such a big cat. No, it came from beside her. From Natalie. Margaret turned to her.

Natalie hissed again and tore off toward the wall across from the desk. The lioness kept pace with her, to the edge of the smoke, and then Natalie alone smashed through the window. A much weightier creature hit the ground by the sound of her crash and then took off to places unknown.

Margaret glanced down at her hands. Her vision remained smudged, even with the smoke dissipating, but the form of the trophy in her hands was unmistakable—the lioness head she had seen mounted on the wall this afternoon. If she got in her car, she could chase after them. Letting Natalie alone out there, without her midnight snack at the fridge? Someone was going to get hurt.

Someone was already hurt. Margaret dropped the taxidermied head and rushed to Heather's side. "Mrs.—Heather, are you okay? Can you speak to me?"

Heather groaned. "Am I okay?"

"That's what I asked."

"I don't think so." Heather reached down her

side. Her hand came back red. "I think I'm dying."

CB

5: A Shade of Gold

Margaret sat in the waiting room outside the emergency room, her head in her hands. She didn't know what had become of Heather yet. The ambulance took her hours ago and she was already in surgery by the time Margaret arrived. She tried to call Heather's sister, but there was no answer at Alicia's house and she hadn't tried again.

She spent the following hours ruminating on her failure, with intervals of sleep here and there. Morning arrived before any news.

A demon had seemed so obvious until it wasn't. Nathaniel's ghost wasn't a bad guess, for everything Heather had suggested. Margaret had considered other options, other kinds of spirits.

With Nathaniel's penchant for world travel, anything was possible.

Margaret hadn't considered possession by animal. She had heard of animal avatars that were welcomed to commune with human hosts as part of religious and spiritual practices. This was different. This was an eleven-year-old girl in the heart of Connecticut, who made the innocent mistake of sitting in her late father's study, likely because she missed him. It wasn't her fault that dead animals lined every nook and cranny of that room.

Which brought Margaret to the recordings. She hadn't had the chance to listen to them until after the ambulance pulled away, after the police finished questioning her, while she decided whether she was going to drive home from the Glasgow house or head to the hospital. Before she listened, the recordings didn't seem like they could tell her much she didn't already know.

She was wrong about that, too. They pushed her to drive to the hospital and warn Heather herself.

"Ms. Margaret Willow?"

Margaret placed her spare spectacles on her face and looked up at a nurse in blue scrubs. Her nametag said Rachel.

"Heather Glasgow is awake," Rachel said. "She's going to make it."

News that should've filled Margaret with ecstasy only gave her the slightest relief. Heather would live. One less thing to feel guilty about.

Rachel led Margaret away from the ER, down another corridor to the post-op room where they had brought Heather Glasgow. "She's only come up from anesthesia minutes ago. We gave her another sedative, and something for her pain because Lord knows she'll need it. You'll only have a few minutes, is what I mean."

"Thank you."

Margaret and Heather needed to have a conversation. Margaret would've liked it later, but in case there was no later, it had to be now. Natalie was missing. Margaret wasn't sure how to help. And then there were the recordings. Heather wouldn't be awake long. Margaret wasn't sure she could say any of this before time ran out.

"Were the two of you at the circus or

71

something?" Rachel asked. "That wound. Some big cat must've done that. A cougar or a lion, right?"

Margaret turned to the open doorway. "I need to talk to Heather. I don't mean to be rude." She stepped into the room, up to Heather's bedside.

Heather lay under a thin sheet. The lioness had gored her left side, under the ribs, likely when they collided beside Nathaniel's desk. Her face was pale, her eyelids heavy.

Margaret leaned over her. "You have your husband's way with animals."

"Don't make me laugh, Ms. Willow. It'll hurt." Heather's hand snatched Margaret's, quick as a snake. The sedative was going to hit her hard. "When they find out what happened, they're going to blame her. Don't let them hurt Natalie."

"I won't if I can help it." Had she guessed at Margaret's uselessness? Had she listened to the recordings herself since last night and hadn't said anything? Margaret doubted that. Now didn't seem the time to tell her.

Heather stared up with warm, wet eyes. "Promise to help her. I'm sorry I rushed it, but it's not her fault. It's her father's, I'm sure of it. That stupid man."

A promise like that was going to be hard to keep at this point. Not making the promise while Heather lay there, her consciousness fading, would've been even harder.

"I promise," Margaret heard herself say. As if she had a choice. Natalie was already deep in a mess. Nothing else Margaret did could make it worse.

"Okay. You promise." Heather's hand let go. "I want to see her draw more animals, Ms. Willow. I want to see her go to high school. I'm parenting for two. I need to see her live her life, and that means she has to live it. Get that thing out of her. Get it out before she kills someone. Before it kills her." Her eyelids slammed shut. "I love her so much."

Margaret stood up from the bed. Heather put it succinctly, didn't she? Get it out of Natalie. Margaret left the hospital bed and found her way back to the waiting room. She could sit there a while longer, but dwelling on her mistakes wasn't going to help Natalie.

There was work to do. Margaret headed for the parking lot and started her car.

The police had been to the Glasgow house, put up their tape, and done some investigating, but no one stood guard in the driveway or at the front door. Had Heather died, things would be different. As it was, this was only an accident with some peculiarities. Anyone searching for Natalie Glasgow only did so out of concern. She had gone missing after her mother suffered a wild animal attack and was only eleven years old, after all.

Margaret parked on the street, same place she left her car last night. Heather's car sat in the driveway. The broken window of Nathaniel's study faced the back of the house, which meant Natalie had started from the ground there and probably kept going in that direction.

Which made it all the stranger when Margaret approached Heather's car and found Natalie asleep in the back seat. Her feet were black with soil, her nightgown torn on her left sleeve, and a few burs stuck to the same shoulder. Her mouth looked clear, but her reddened fingernails said she might have eaten in the night.

Margaret opened one door, rolled down a window, and closed the door. Best to let Natalie sleep while she decided what to do with her.

It would be smart to call the police. Let them know where Natalie was, where they could take her off the street so she wouldn't hurt anyone else. That was blood on her fingers, under her nails, no doubt about it. A rabbit? A bird? Something larger? Margaret clasped her hands. Something Margaret-sized?

If she called the police, they would bring Natalie to the hospital, where her mother couldn't hide her any longer. Night would come and then Natalie would give them a reason to lock her up. She wouldn't be able to hurt anyone else. She also wouldn't get any better.

Out here, maybe there was a solution to be found. If they detained Natalie, was there a judge in this world who would let Margaret and her colleagues perform some archaic ritual? She doubted there was one who would even let a priest perform an exorcism. The old ways were nonsense in the days of the new ways unless they could be exploited.

Which meant if she called the police, Natalie would spend the rest of her life in an asylum. The lioness would eventually wear her out and kill her from the inside.

Margaret stepped through the unlocked front door and paused in the living room. She looked up at the second floor stairway. Natalie had spent most of her time in her bedroom throughout this ordeal, but that wasn't where the ordeal began. Margaret headed for the study, where yellow police tape crossed the shattered door. She opened the other door and slipped inside.

The room remained as she left it—the salt circle, the snuffed candles, the blackened bundle of spruce. The saucer remained intact, but the belladonna was nothing but shriveled pulp. A key with a one-time use.

Outside the circle lay the lioness's head on a wooden mount. Nearby, a partial paw print smudged the salt. Margaret supposed that could be misinterpreted for anything, but she'd seen the lioness cross the circle. She was present. Perhaps if not for the smoke she would've been trapped behind lines of salt.

She picked up the head and placed it back on the wall where it had been mounted yesterday. If the lioness wanted anything, it wasn't this head. The head had warded her off. Was the spirit bent on revenge or did the lioness have a stake in this beyond her own demise at the hands of Nathaniel Glasgow?

"Your body." Margaret glanced over the walls. "What does a man do with a lion's body when he only wants the head?"

She imagined in many cases where lions were part of the ecosystem, the lion was eaten, either by hungry people or scavenging animals. A call to the taxidermist wasn't out of the question. She would have to hope he was still in business and that Nathaniel kept his number in a rolodex, perhaps knocked off the desk last night.

A step toward the desk made glass crunch beneath her foot. She leaned back on her heel, expecting to find her spectacles from last night, even more broken than before.

Instead she found the framed photo of Nathaniel, his foot proudly planted on a wildebeest. No wildebeest prize graced the study.

Maybe it wasn't impressive enough to him or he couldn't drag it back to the States. Or maybe it was only bait for another hunt. Hence, the photo. It had to be a compulsion for him, a means of mastering the world. He might have expected that when he was gone, the study left intact, that people would step through those double doors and his wife would show them the marvel that was her husband.

"Nothing on this Earth that man couldn't find and kill," Heather might say, if she was a different kind of person. Her words to Margaret when they first entered the study told a different story. Heather was embarrassed by this room, afraid it made her husband out to look like something worse than he was.

And she had no idea how bad it was. Margaret knew. She had listened to the recordings. At first they played only snippets of her conversation with Heather from inside Heather's bedroom. Then there was Natalie's door and Natalie herself, and the weight of the lioness she carried through the house.

But there were other sounds. They began with

insects in the distance, a foreign-sounding cicada cacophony. It might've sounded normal if this wasn't autumn. There was no rationalizing the other sounds. An elephant's cry. Galloping hooves, maybe gazelle, maybe zebra. A bear, a hissing crocodile, birds of all kinds.

"I don't know why you had such a potent draw," Margaret said to the photograph. "I've never seen it so bad. Everything you killed became a frayed yarn ball of fury, ready to snag anything it touched after you died. Even here, even with me. How can I know I'm not being exposed to any of these poor animals right now?"

A color caught her eye. She peered closer at the photo.

And then she saw it. She saw it, knew that shade of gold, and remembered what Heather told her about it, if it was the same. It had to be the same.

"If I'm right." Margaret set the frame down on the messy floor. "Please, I have to be right this time."

She couldn't leave Natalie to be found. She would have to come with, maybe get some water in her, take her to the restroom at some gas station on the way. They couldn't delay too long. It was morning now, but eventually it would be night again.

Margaret returned to the living room with her bag. Most of what she brought to the Glasgow house last night was useless here now, but she had her own book of numbers and addresses. She picked up the receiver for Heather's rotary phone on the wall and began her calls.

First she called Trish at home and told her she wouldn't make it for supper again, and perhaps not to expect her until morning. She left out the severity of the situation.

Second, Margaret called Alicia again. This time, she answered. Margaret told her not to ask questions, but that she needed information and Heather wasn't in a state to answer. Alicia told her what she needed to know and she told Alicia what hospital to find Heather.

Last, because Margaret couldn't get the recordings out of her head, she gave Alicia instructions, and to either have Heather carry them out after she recovered, or for Alicia to carry them out herself. Someone had to take responsibility and Margaret couldn't be sure she was coming back from this.

"Take everything Nathaniel ever brought to the Glasgow house from afar, pile it up in the backyard, and burn it at sunset." Burning would sanctify. Burning would free anything that shouldn't have been there.

She didn't elaborate. There wasn't time. The sun had been up for too long already.

CR

6: Graveyard Dirt

The sky had grown graciously overcast by the time Margaret arrived at her destination. Natalie stirred in the backseat as they pulled through the front gates, her voice a childlike whimper. Margaret had made sure to give her some water and help her to a gas station restroom on the way, but if she wet the backseat while Margaret worked, so be it. There wasn't time to babysit her.

The car parked on a grassy patch not far from where Alicia had directed. Margaret would've liked nothing more than to sit in the car and talk to Natalie. Easier to make promises than keep them, but if she didn't keep this promise, sitting in this car was going to become lethally unpleasant by nightfall.

"It's illegal," Margaret said. "And sometimes considered blasphemous, but less often than you might think. In your case it won't be immoral. Still." She reached over the seat and caressed Natalie's head. A feverish warmth cooked her skin. "This thing inside you is angry. I can't blame her."

Margaret stepped out of the car, locked it, and grabbed a shovel out of the trunk. Then she stepped across the grass.

Heather said Nathaniel had a favorite hat. Margaret presumed it was the hat in the photograph, a hat the same color as the lioness's fur. Perhaps—hopefully likely—this was what the lioness wanted. And where was that hat? Heather had told Margaret yesterday afternoon.

"Nathaniel Adam Glasgow," Margaret read aloud. The headstone was a black block of clean slate. The dry flowers at its base had been there for maybe a month. "Husband, Father, Traveler. May He Roam Heaven as He Roamed the Earth." She drove the head of the shovel into the earth, grown over with faded grass.

Margaret had performed strange activities and rituals as a midwife, or a witch, whatever you wanted to call her. She'd taken soil from graves before, with permission, and only to help people. Never in her life had she unearthed a grave in a race against the sun.

Nathaniel was a few feet down. Since he died of heart failure and not some horrific accident, Margaret could assume he had an open wake or funeral, which meant the top half of his casket would open on its own. She would only need to dig up his upper half. More of him would have to be dug up just so she could reach that far down, but the soil could form a slope rather than a six-foot long rectangle.

Hours of digging dragged by. Two feet down. Three feet down. The work itself was dull, but time was short. The day dragged on, yet every hour gone was an hour more she wished she had. Now and then, she glanced back at her car. The doors remained closed. Natalie was harmless in the daylight. Margaret wished to get in the car and leave. Her mind hung back in Heather's bedroom, sweating, her nerves on fire, dreading what was to come.

It didn't occur to her until the mid-afternoon that the graveyard was far more dangerous than the Glasgow kitchen. Natalie would awaken with the lioness inside her when the sun set wherever she was, but here in this place of death, there were no promises that the lioness herself wouldn't manifest like in the study.

Margaret grasped a clump of soil from her pile and let the grains sift through her fingers. "Never underestimate the power of graveyard dirt." That power went both ways. She could have used it in her ritual last night, but the belladonna seemed more welcoming to a departed family member. It also gave strength to the presence of the dead.

Gloom overtook the sky prematurely thanks to the overcast. A trick of the light, maybe, but more likely the day would soon end and Margaret wasn't done. She hunched atop the lower half of where the coffin would be and thrust shovelful after shovelful of soil out of the hole. There had to be a bottom to this.

She couldn't help but stand up straight to

glance at her car. The windows were beginning to fog. Heather had warned on Margaret's first night that she couldn't set a watch to Natalie's episodes.

"It's just from Natalie's breathing." Margaret returned to digging. She couldn't be too far from Nathaniel's casket. She began to dig in one spot so that she could reach the casket's lid sooner and confirm how far down she still had to go, or how short she was going to fall from finding that hat before—

The car squeaked. Margaret couldn't help herself. She glanced back again.

White mist painted most of the windshield.

Margaret returned to digging. "It's going to be a chilly night. Natalie's body heat is just warming the car." Her tone was dismissive, as if what she said was harmless, but she was painfully right. Natalie's body heat became its own atmosphere at night and it was filling her car as night drew near.

The shovel hit a firm surface. Margaret exhaled so hard it came out as a guffaw. Then she gritted her teeth and growled, and her digging grew frantic. She was close in one spot, so she was close all around that spot. She just needed to clear the coffin's upper half. Another fifty or so shovelfuls, maybe.

Her car squeaked again. Now the windshield and fellow windows were completely clouded up, obscuring the inside like the smoke of burning spruce wood. The sky eased into a quieter, darker hue.

"I won't look again," Margaret promised herself. "That's a promise I'm keeping for me. Natalie, sweetie, please wait. Please."

She plowed her shovel to the side of the casket. Blisters dotted her palms. Her arms weren't willing to dig much longer. That was fine—she didn't have much longer to make them dig. She was beginning to see the perimeter of the casket.

Her tires groaned, the car being jostled from the inside. Natalie's body could manage her bedroom doorknob even with the lioness inside her, but maybe not car door locks. The next sound Margaret heard was a hand or foot or paw breaking one of her back windows.

She kept her mouth shut now, breathing as

soft as she could while she continued to dig. The casket lid was almost clear enough to open. If she was quiet, perhaps the lioness would hunt elsewhere in the empty cemetery. Margaret could dig and breathe and sweat in peace.

Sweat. She'd been digging most of the day and sweated through most of it. Her blazer hung from the side of Nathaniel's headstone, a blazer she'd already used to distract Natalie another night. Body and clothing reeked together. The lioness would smell it, sure as she smelled it last night and the night before.

Stiff, dry grass crunched beneath heavy steps.

Margaret fell to her hands and knees and swept at the lid of the casket. One hand fumbled for a latch. A simple, brass-colored clasp held the casket shut on the right side. She tugged, but it wouldn't budge. There wasn't time to figure out how to open it. She stood again, lifted her shovel high, and drove the head down on the lock. The clashing metal sang loud as a dinner bell.

If Natalie drew closer, Margaret didn't hear her now. The lioness could be quiet too, like the other night when she crossed from kitchen to stairs. Wouldn't want to alarm her prey. As if Margaret could crawl out of this hole fast enough to outrun a hungry, undead predator.

Only the ache in her legs and the stinging across her hands kept her from turning to useless jelly. Her fingers clawed at the edge of the casket and thrust it open. The smell hit her strong. She had to press her face into her arm and hide a cough. When she leaned over the open casket again, there was heat across her back. She didn't dare look, not after keeping her promise this far.

Nathaniel had been dead ten months. Long enough to decompose, not long enough to be a skeleton. There was no hat on his head.

A growl rumbled just above. It quaked through Margaret's bones and the dewy bones beneath her. She broke her promise to herself. There was Natalie, standing in her dreamlike stupor, the way she stood at the fridge that first night.

And at her side, head leaned down into the grave, stood the lioness, her golden gaze fixed on Margaret. The one who got away twice now. She would pounce tonight. She would feed.

Into the coffin. The thought turned Margaret's stomach, but if she clambered inside with the body and closed the lid, she would be safe until pre-dawn when Natalie's episode passed. The casket had to stand against all the earth. It could resist four hundred pounds of muscle and fury. It had to.

Margaret pressed her hands against Nathaniel's clothes and his chest gave way beneath her. "It's your fault," she said. "You were supposed to have the hat. You did this to your family."

The lioness tensed. Margaret didn't have to look. She could feel those muscles, feel that black frown on the lioness's snout curl open into a hungry maw. Saliva dripped onto the nape of Margaret's neck, into her soiled hair. The lioness was practically alive tonight among the mounds of earth. Perhaps even Margaret had underestimated the power of the graveyard soil to unite the worlds of the living and the dead.

Her hands pawed across Nathaniel, pressed him to the side to make room. The stink made Margaret's head swim. She couldn't pass out here, no matter how exhausted and overwhelmed, not

91

with the lioness above her. Her arm stretched into the lower half of the coffin.

Bristly fur stabbed at the blisters on her palm.

Of course Nathaniel didn't wear the hat on his head. That would have looked crass at the wake and the funeral, as if the man's pride was more important than his family's mourning. The hat was tucked into the side of the casket, gently, lovingly. Margaret's fingers seized it and tore back from inside the casket.

"I have it!" she snapped. She saw it for the first time as she sat up. That beautiful golden color, twisted into an ugly little round hat, the hair trailing down a little as if it was a coonskin cap made of lion.

On the slope of soil, the lioness hunched her back. About to strike. About to maul.

Margaret forced herself to stand. She thrust the hat at the lioness's face. That golden gaze shined beyond the hat. The lioness didn't understand. Her spirit obeyed instinct, and that instinct said hunt and feed, nothing more.

"This is what you wanted. Take it." Margaret stumbled over the open casket. She was about to die. She knew it sure as the lioness knew she was about to eat. This wasn't that night in the kitchen with Natalie and the crucifix, when untold possibilities stirred in the darkness. This was a surety. She owed a hundred apologies and wouldn't have the chance to give a single one.

She pressed the hat only inches from the lioness's face. The lioness inhaled its scent and neither she nor Margaret knew the graveyard anymore.

❧

All she knows is the heat today.

It is immense. It is greater than hunger. She cannot wait for the others to return. She must drink. It is not a hunt. She is sloppy, but she only understands this later.

At the watering hole, the prey-beasts continue to drink despite her presence. She is not close, but not far. She is not interested in them and they know it. If one of the pride can be seen, then she is not a threat. If she wished to be a threat, she would not be seen. Always fear one of the pride that is unseen, as if she is always there.

One creature does not respect the ways of the

watering hole. It is not a starving hyena and not an elephant in heatstroke. It is a man-beast. She has seen his kind before and knows the terrible fire and earth they spit from afar. He sees all there is to see at the watering hole, or so he thinks. He sees her, yes. He does not see her see him.

When he tries to sneak, when he tries to kill too close, she is on him. She comes to drink. Had he come to drink, she would have let him, but he comes to kill. So she must kill.

Or try to. The man-beast knows her kind. His fire and earth pierce her foreleg when she pounces at him. Her claw rips his chest, her teeth find his arm. Another peal of thunder puts his fire into her low places. This tells her to leave, but not before she's taken a small piece from one limb. Then she disappears into the brush, her thirst not sated, her blood sating the thirst of the earth. She is dying.

She wants to go home. To wander is more important, to not lead the man-beast back to her. She believes the man-beast to be like one of the pride in this, to chase the weary, the injured, the sick across the grasses, to devour the prey.

The man-beast is different. She learns this

only when her long, wayward travel finds her home. By then, she is weak with lost blood, with thirst. The sun above is merciless. Merciless as the man-beast.

The man-beast did not follow her trail of blood, but instead found the path she took to reach the watering hole and followed it to where she came from. To home. To where she left her three small ones.

They are missing.

If the man-beast's fire was not killing her, she believes she might stay. Lost cubs can be replaced if their mother lives. Except she does not want to replace them. They were hers. They were the first she had and now the last. The male she made them with was young and soon driven from the pride by a stranger. Many nights she hid her small ones from this strange male. She took great pain to keep them alive in this world.

She cannot let them go. So, she begins to walk. The man-beast can track. She can track, too. She tracks his steps and the trails of the monstrous wheeled creatures that the man-beasts ride. He leads her through the grass and into a place where the man-beasts gather. There are young she can easily feed on, but she is not here for feeding. She is here for revenge.

The other man-beasts cry out when she enters their nest. The man-beast who stole her young hears the warning, is expecting her. He readies to spit fire and earth, the same that is killing her but has not killed her yet.

Again, she does not understand the ways of the man-beasts. They are not like the prey-beasts, and most importantly, they are not like the pride.

It is her small ones who give her pause. It is her small ones who kill her. They lay on a table. The man-beast has killed them.

If she understood the language of the man-beasts, she would hear that they had no intent to kill her small ones. They want cubs alive. There was an accident. A fall, because the man-beast who is killing her was too weak to carry the bag he stowed them in. She cannot comprehend. There is only heat and rage, thirst and starvation, and deep inside, an emotion she can barely understand. All those nights she protected them, only for their lives to end in this. She wants a greater destiny for her young. Too late. All for nothing.

The man-beast erupts and she feels the fire and earth again, this time through her neck. Blood cakes the fur down her limbs, her belly, and now it crosses her face. She watches the small ones' faces. They are the last thing she sees in the living world.

And what comes after is hunger, fear, and hatred. She can see nothing else.

∞

The lioness retreated from the edge of the hole. Nathaniel's cap lay idle in the soil. The lioness growled low. Three mewling throats answered her. Where there were once only four legs, now three lion cubs circled and nuzzled.

Margaret stood steady and cautious. She remained fixed under that golden gaze, but the force of it slackened. The lioness looked confused, as if she hadn't known what she was doing, hadn't even remembered she birthed little ones or what happened to them when their mother crossed paths with Nathaniel Glasgow.

Natalie moaned. Margaret clambered up out of the hole just in time to catch her before she went careening into her father's grave. She pulled Natalie back from the edge, across the soil mounds, and held onto her tight.

Natalie nestled her face into Margaret's chest and began to cry. They were the same racking sobs as her mother.

"It's alright," Margaret whispered. "Everything's okay now. You're safe. Let it out. Good girl. You'll be okay." Over and over, as many times as Natalie needed to hear it, as many times as Margaret could say it. She rocked Natalie back and forth.

Her attention returned to the lioness and her cubs.

The lioness finally turned from her and Natalie. She pressed her face against each of her cubs and breathed deep the scent of them. They purred beneath her, chased at each other, no memory of what had happened to them.

Margaret hoped the same for Natalie.

The lioness uttered a rumbling purr and ushered the cubs ahead of her. They began to pad along, still playing, but headed east. Their mother brought up the rear, where she could keep an eye on them. Tonight and last night, she stalked with each step, a predator on the hunt. Now she strolled peaceably, her long tail swatting back and forth.

Behind her, she dragged a strip of fleshy material the way a hurried shoe might drag an unnoticed errant strip of toilet paper out of the restroom.

Margaret grasped Natalie's head tight to her chest in case the girl stopped crying and tried to look. She couldn't have her seeing this.

It was Nathaniel Glasgow. Part of him. No muscle, no inner tissue, no bones. He was only a skin, dragged by his leg at the hind foot of the lioness, an unmoving, powerless shadow.

Almost all skin, a hide stripped from a body. On his face, most of it caved-in where a skull would have been in life, to the side of his now-shriveled hawkish nose, Nathaniel still had one wide eye. It looked this way and that, alert and pleading. No other part of him could move. It fixed a desperate stare on Margaret, or maybe on sobbing Natalie, but that was all it could do. Glance and stare and be dragged by the lioness.

Margaret stared back at him. He wanted help.

It was outside her power to give. Everything he killed became a frayed yarn ball of fury, ready to snag anything it touched after he died.

Perhaps even himself.

She watched his tearful eye until the lioness pulled him too far away in the dark to be seen. Her golden visage remained a moment longer, but then that, too, faded into the darkness with her three cubs.

A cool breeze set in across the graveyard and Natalie began to shiver in Margaret's arms.

It was going to be a chilly night.

附

About the Author

Hailey Piper grew up in the haunted woods of New York, where she began her obsession with monsters, ghosts, and all things that go bump in the night. She and her wife live Maryland, where she keeps her childhood nightmares alive by writing them down.

She is a member of the Horror Writers Association, and her short fiction appears in Daily Science Fiction, The Arcanist, Flash Fiction Online, *Year's Best Hardcore Horror*.

THE POSSESSION OF NATALIE GLASGOW is her debut novella.

Visit www.haileypiper.com to keep an ear to the ground on what Hailey is working on, or follow her on Twitter via @HaileyPiperSays.

Content warning:

This book contains depictions of violence toward animals.

Lightning Source UK Ltd.
Milton Keynes UK
UKHW010630260821
389510UK00001B/127